lithgow palooza readers

Drop, Drip, an Underwater Trip

By Susan Blackaby

School Specialty Publishing

Text Copyright © 2007 School Specialty Publishing. Manatee Character © 2003 by John Lithgow. Manatee Illustration © 2003 by Ard Hoyt.

Printed in the United States of America. All rights reserved. Except as permitted under the United States Copyright Act, no part of this publication may be reproduced or distributed in any form or by any means, or stored in a database or retrieval system, without prior written permission from the publisher, unless otherwise indicated.

Library of Congress Cataloging-in-Publication Data is on file with the publisher.

Send all inquiries to:
School Specialty Publishing
8720 Orion Place
Columbus, OH 43240-2111

ISBN 0-7696-4253-5

1 2 3 4 5 6 7 8 9 10 PHXBK 12 11 10 09 08 07 06

Table of Contents

Fish 4–5
Mammals .6–7
Birds 8–9
Amphibians and Reptiles 10–11
Invertebrates 12–13
Tide Pool 14–15
Coral Reef 16–17
Estuary and Open Water 18–19
Aquarium Workers 20–25
Aquariums 26–29
Thinking About It 31–32

Fish

At an **aquarium**, you can see fish up close.
See the scales that cover a fish's body.
See the gills that help a fish breathe.
See the fins that help a fish swim.
An aquarium is home to fish
of all colors, shapes, and sizes.

Manatee Mentions
Aquariums have both freshwater tanks and saltwater tanks.

Mammals

At an aquarium, you can see mammals in water.
Watch manatees swim.
Watch dolphins dive.
See orcas jump out of the water and crash down again.
See beavers and muskrats splash in water that is not deep.

Manatee Mentions
Most aquariums have beach **habitats** and stream habitats for mammals.

Birds

Some aquariums have birds
that live near water.
You can see puffins and pelicans.
You can see gulls and geese.
You can watch birds with long legs
wade through water.
You can watch birds with webbed feet
swim and splash.

Manatee Mentions
Some aquariums have rainforest **exhibits** with toucans like this one.

Amphibians and Reptiles

Aquariums also have water creatures that hop, slither, and creep. These creatures are amphibians and reptiles. You can see frogs and toads. You can see snakes and alligators. You can see tiny turtles and giant tortoises.

Manatee Mentions
Sea turtles at an aquarium need both water for swimming and land for nesting.

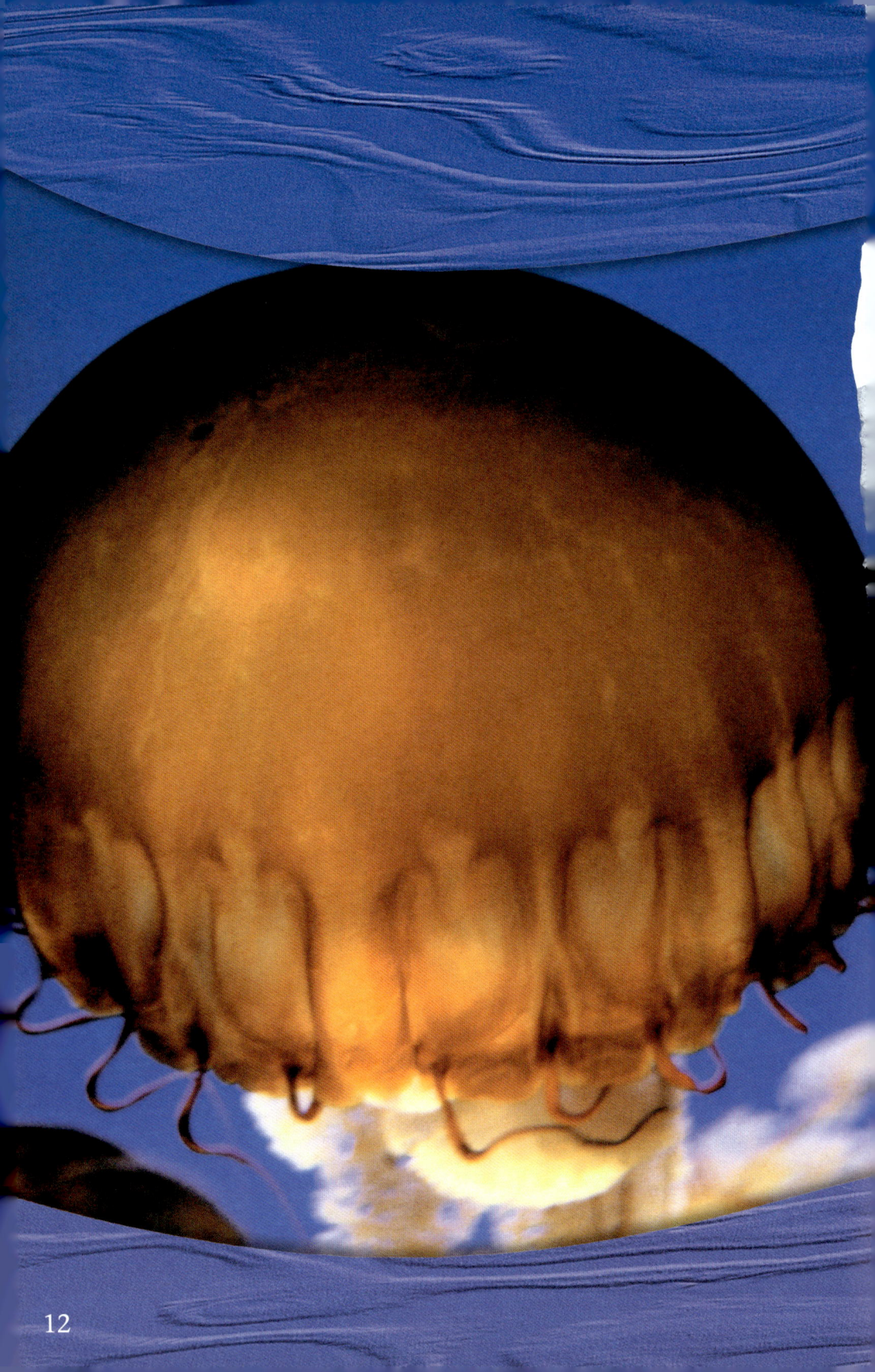

Invertebrates

Aquariums have crabs, shrimp, and lobsters.
They have sea urchins and starfish.
They have clams, snails, and octopuses.
All of these animals are **invertebrates** that live in water.
They do not have backbones.

Manatee Mentions

About 95 percent of a jellyfish's body is water. They have no bones, brains, hearts, lungs, or blood.

Tide Pool

At an aquarium, you may see
a tide pool exhibit.
You can study the animals
that live there.
Sea slugs and sea anemones
cling to the rocks.
So do snails and mussels.
Waves crash over the pool
when the tide is high.
The sun beats down on it
when the tide is low.

Manatee Mentions

A tide pool is like its own mini ocean world. You can see animals eating, hunting, and fighting in a tide pool.

Coral Reef

Some aquariums have **coral reef** exhibits.
A coral reef is like an underwater ridge or mound.
It is made from the dead bodies of millions of tiny sea creatures.
A coral reef is an **ecosystem**.
It is home to many forms of sea life.

Manatee Mentions
A coral reef in an aquarium looks just like a real one. But it is a man-made model built for the exhibit.

Estuary and Open Water

Some aquariums have **estuary** exhibits.
They show fish and mammals
that live in bays.
They show birds and reptiles
that live in **wetlands**.
Some aquariums also have
open-water exhibits.
They show marine animals, such as
whales, that live in deep water.

Manatee Mentions
Some coastal aquariums have real-world exhibits. The Monterey Bay Aquarium in California features seals that live in Monterey Bay.

Aquarium Workers

There are lots of jobs to do at an aquarium.
Model-makers build the exhibits.
They work with scientists to set up ecosystems.
The habitats they make are just like real ones.
The marine animals that live in them must feel right at home.

Manatee Mentions
Scuba divers clean the exhibit tanks and feed the marine animals.

Trainers work closely with
marine animals.
They keep the animals calm and safe.
They teach the animals to do tricks.
They study the animals' habits.
A **veterinarian** keeps
the animals healthy.
Some workers teach classes
about sea creatures to visitors.

Manatee Mentions

Many aquariums have hundreds of volunteers. The volunteers do everything from teaching visitors about animals to preparing food for animals to eat.

Aquariums also have science labs. Scientists test the water in the tanks. They study the marine animals. They work on **conservation**. They find ways to save animals that need help.

Manatee Mentions

Many jobs at an aquarium take place behind the scenes. For example, a writer writes all of the information for exhibit posters and signs.

Aquariums

Aquariums exhibit everything from snails to whales.
Some aquariums, such as The Parker Manatee Aquarium in Florida, house only certain animals.
Some aquariums collect many different kinds of marine animals.
The Monterey Bay Aquarium in California is home to thousands of different animals.

Manatee Mentions
You can visit The National Aquarium, shown above, in Baltimore, Maryland. It has more than 560 different kinds of animals.

Dive into the deep blue sea.
Tour the world of a tide pool.
Explore a coral reef.
Investigate islands and inlets.
Wade through wetlands.
Discover new worlds
at your local aquarium!

Manatee Mentions

An aquarium is the perfect place to let your imagination run wild.

Vocabulary

aquarium–a building that holds a collection of fish and other water animals. *Our class visited the aquarium.*

conservation–the protection of animals and the wise use of resources. *The conservation of manatees will help them survive.*

coral reef–an underwater ridge made of the skeletons of tiny sea creatures. *The coral reef stretched for hundreds of miles along the coast.*

ecosystem–a community made up of the plants and animals that live in a particular place. *A wetland is an ecosystem made up of plants, animals, and water.*

estuary–a place where a river meets the ocean. *The seals swam in the estuary.*

exhibit–something shown; a display. *We saw a toucan in the tropical rain forest exhibit.*

freshwater–water that is not salty. *A beaver lives in freshwater.*

habitat–a place where a plant or animal naturally grows and lives. *A dolphin lives in a saltwater habitat.*

invertebrate–without a backbone. *The jellyfish is an invertebrate.*

scuba–equipment that allows a diver to breathe underwater. *John wore scuba gear to explore the coral reef.*

veterinarian–a doctor who cares for animals. *The veterinarian gave the otter some medicine.*

wetland–a low-lying water habitat, such as a marsh or swamp. *In a wetland, you might see a manatee.*

Think About It!

1. What do fish use to breathe underwater?
2. Which marine animals would you see in a tide pool exhibit?
3. Which marine animals might be in an open water exhibit?
4. What kinds of animals do not have backbones? What are these animals called?
5. What types of jobs are there at an aquarium?

The Story and You!

1. Which aquarium exhibit from the book would you most like to see? Why?
2. Which marine animal would you most like to see? Why?
3. How is your home like an ecosystem?
4. If you owned an aquarium, which animals would you exhibit?
5. What kind of job would you like to have at an aquarium? Why?